# Saint
# Colmcille

## (Also known as Saint Columba)

This story was adapted by author Rod Smith
and illustrated by Derry Dillon

IRELAND'S BEST KNOWN STORIES
IN A NUTSHELL

*To all my nieces, nephews, grandnieces and grandnephews.*
*Hello to Jasmine and Zara O'Brien, and special thanks also to the Dooley family.*

Published 2018
Poolbeg Press Ltd

123 Grange Hill, Baldoyle
Dublin 13, Ireland

Text © Poolbeg Press Ltd 2018

A catalogue record for this book is available from the British Library.

ISBN 978 1 78199 843 4

Cover design and illustrations by Derry Dillon
Printed by GPS Colour Graphics Ltd

# This book belongs to

------------------------------------------------

## Also in the Nutshell series

***Early Life***

The year was 520. In an area called Gartan,
County Donegal, the powerful Cenél Conaill family
celebrated the latest addition to the family – a baby
boy. His mother Eithne cradled him in her arms.

"I had a dream about you, my little treasure," she whispered to the child. "I was visited by an angel who gave me a beautiful robe. Then he took it away from me and the robe flew into the air and grew larger until it covered the whole countryside. Then the angel spoke to me: '*Do not be upset – you will have a child who will lead many souls to heaven.*'"

Just then, a neighbour came in to see the child.

"He's a grand lad to be sure, and sure why wouldn't he be? With a father who's one of the powerful O'Neills, his mother a Leinster princess and his great-great-grandfather the High King of Ireland, Niall of the Nine Hostages!"

Eithne smiled at her husband Fedelmid when the neighbour left.

"There's as much a chance of me being a princess of Leinster as you being related to Niall of the Nine Hostages!" she said with a laugh.

"Well, you'll always be my princess!" Fedelmid replied.

They called the baby Crimthann, which is an Irish word meaning "fox". He spent much of his youth praying and meditating and became known as Colum Cille (later spelt Colmcille) which means "dove of the church". Later in life, his own monks knew him as Columba, a Latin word meaning "dove".

When Colmcille was young he was sent away to be brought up and educated by a priest called Cruithnechán, who lived near Kilmacrennan in Donegal.

One night, as Colmcille slept, Cruithnechán was returning from the church when he saw his house full of bright light. When he entered the house, he saw a ball of fire above Colmcille's bed.

The Holy Spirit has shown great favour to this boy, he thought as he bowed down in wonder.

So Colmcille grew up, studying Latin and learning about Christianity. He also learnt how to copy and illustrate manuscripts with marvellous pictures of humans, birds, animals, angels and legendary beasts like dragons. (There was no printing press in those days to print books!)

When he was old enough he became a monk and later a priest, and lived very happily – studying, reading, creating wonderful books, visiting other monasteries and teaching his community about Christianity.

But that happy life was to change.

*A Deadly Disagreement*

In the year 560 Colmcille visited a monk called Saint
Finnian. While he was there he found a beautiful
manuscript of Psalms from the Bible that Finnian had
brought from Rome. He decided to make a copy of it
for himself in secret, as he was afraid he would not
get permission to do so if he asked. Finnian found out
about this, but waited until Colmcille had finished the
manuscript.

"I did not grant you permission to make this copy. Give it to me!" he then demanded.

After working so hard to copy the book, Colmcille refused. He then appealed his case to the High King of Ireland, Diarmait MacCearbhaill.

"Colmcille, you must give this copy to Finnian," the king declared. "*Le gach boin a boinín, le gach leabhar a leabhrán* – to every cow her calf, and to every book its copy."

Colmcille had to hand over the manuscript.

But he soon clashed again with the king on a much more deadly matter. During a disagreement in a hurling match, Curnan, son of the King of Connacht, struck King Diarmait's steward and accidentally killed him.

Curnan ran to Colmcille for help.

"I will grant you sanctuary here in my church," said Colmcille. "No king or soldiers will dare touch you if you claim sanctuary." In those days not even a king would dare ignore the right of sanctuary even if it was claimed by a criminal.

King Diarmait's soldiers arrived and insisted that Colmcille hand over Curnan.

"I will not hand him over to you!" said Colmcille. "He claims sanctuary!"

But the soldiers dragged Curnan outside where he was executed.

Colmcille was horrified. He travelled to the north-west of Ireland where his family, the O'Neills, lived. Then the O'Neills and the King of Connacht (the father of Curnan) fought a battle against Diarmait in 561 at Cúl Dreimhe, Drumcliffe, near Ben Bulben in Sligo. Diarmait's army suffered huge losses while the O'Neills lost just one soldier in the battle.

Colmcille felt huge guilt at the great loss of life in the battle. The role he played in causing the battle was condemned even by his friends and Church leaders met to discuss throwing him out of the Church completely.

Saint Brendan spoke up. "We should not judge this man so harshly," he said. "I have had a vision from God that Colmcille has been chosen by Him to be a great Church leader."

The Church leaders agreed not to punish Colmcille.

*Iona*

After that, Colmcille decided to leave Ireland to travel to Scotland to spread the word of God.

He sailed from Derry in 562 with his assistant Diormit and eleven other companions.

"The people are sad that you are going," Diormit told his master.

"My heart is heavy at the thought of leaving. For my last night in dear Ireland, I lay on the *Leac na Cumha* ("The Flagstone of Loneliness") near my native Gartan," Colmcille replied.

As they travelled down Lough Foyle they were followed by seagulls and birds. "See how the seagulls and birds follow us," said Diormit. "They too cry with grief that you are leaving Ireland."

There is a Scottish legend that says Colmcille and Saint Mo Luag (also known as Lugaid) both intended to build a monastery on the Scottish island of Lismore, so they decided to have a boat race. Colmcille was leading and about to reach the island when Mo Luag cut off his finger and threw it onto the island, which meant he reached the island first. This was a very dramatic (and painful) way to claim the island!

Eventually Colmcille and his group arrived at the remote island of Iona, off the western Scottish coast. He built a monastery there, and became the leader or abbot of the monks who devoted themselves to prayer, study and physical work. Iona soon became a place of great learning.

Colmcille lived very simply. He used a rock as a bed and a large stone as a pillow. When he died the stone pillow was used to mark his grave.

Colmcille became great friends with the two main tribes in Scotland at the time – the Picts and the Dalriada. He persuaded the king of the Picts, Brude Mac Maelchan, to convert to Christianity and he helped to bring peace when there was a fight between Brude and King Conall of the Dalriada.

When King Conall died, such was the trust and respect shown to Colmcille, it was left to him to decide who should become the new king.

***Prophecies and Miracles***

There are many tales about Colmcille's ability to fore-tell the future.

Once, King Áedán of the Dalriada asked Colmcille which of his three eldest sons would succeed him as king. Áedán had at least seven sons at the time.

"None of these will succeed you," Colmcille replied. "Send in your younger sons to me. The one who runs into my arms will succeed you as king."

A son called Eochaid Buide ran to the saint as soon as he entered the room.

"This child will be the next king," said Colmcille.

This came to pass as the three eldest sons were killed in battle.

Another time, Colmcille told a man visiting him that he must return home immediately. That the place was under attack.

"My wife and children!" the man exclaimed.

"They are safe. Your possessions have been stolen, but you'll find your family hiding on the mountainside."

When the man returned home he found this to be true.

It is said that Colmcille also performed many miracles.

One day he stayed as an overnight guest of a poor man called Colmán. The next morning the saint asked the man about his wealth.

"I only have five little cows," Colmán replied.

Colmcille blessed the cows. "You will have one hundred and five cows for you and your family." The herd grew to this number, and never exceeded one hundred and five.

Colmcille was visited once by a poor man who could not feed his family.

"Fetch me a stick of wood from the forest," the saint said.

Colmcille sharpened the stick, blessed it and gave it to the man.

"This stick will not kill any people or cattle but it will kill wild animals and fish for you and your family so that you never need to go hungry again."

For a time the man used the stick and his family were never hungry. However, he was warned by others that the stick was so sharp it might harm a person. So, despite the fact that Colmcille had said it wouldn't, he chopped up the stick and burned it, and never had a steady supply of food for his family from that day on. He was forced to return to begging for food.

Another time, in the province of the Picts, Colmcille went to the house of a family who were very upset as one of their children had died.

"Bring me to where the boy lies and leave me alone with him," the saint commanded.

Colmcille knelt by the boy. As he prayed tears fell from his eyes, for he too was very upset at the death of the boy.

"Wake up again and stand on your feet," he commanded.

The boy opened his eyes and stood up. He was returned to his family and there were great celebrations.

## The Loch Ness Monster

One day, while travelling in Scotland, Colmcille and his group had to cross the River Ness. They came across a funeral of a man who had been killed by a mysterious creature in the river. Colmcille needed a small boat that was on the other side of the shore and, to the surprise of everyone, asked one of the group to swim over to the other side to fetch it. As he was swimming across, a beast suddenly rose to the surface. Colmcille raised his hand in the air and, making the Sign of the Cross, shouted at the creature: "*Go no further! Do not touch that man! Go back at once!*" The creature immediately went back under the water. This is thought to be one of the first sightings of the mysterious Loch Ness Monster.

### *Colmcille helps the Poets*

Colmcille had also trained as a poet. In his later years, he attended a meeting of kings at Druim Cett, near Limavady, County Derry. One of the issues discussed was the role of poets, called filidh in Irish. These filidh were an ancient group who had great skill in writing poetry and history, and wrote verses that praised their masters. However, over the years they demanded more and more from kings and leaders in return for their services. Eventually the kings decided they were going to expel all of the poets.

Colmcille spoke on their behalf. He agreed that they had become too powerful. He proposed that the filidh should remain, but as a smaller group with less privileges. This was agreed and the poets were very grateful to Colmcille for his help.

*The Death of Colmcille*

By May 593, Colmcille was in his mid-seventies. He decided to visit the monks who were working on the other side of Iona. He knew he was dying and wanted to visit them one more time.

"My friends … this is the last time you will see my face here," he told them.

His fellow monks were very sad on hearing this news.

"Be of good cheer, my children. God bless you all here, and all who dwell on this island of Iona."

A few days later, Colmcille went with his servant Diormit to the barn to bless the grain which they used to bake bread.

"I am very glad that you will have enough bread for a year if I have to go away," he said.

"Father, you make us very sad as you keep speaking about your death," Diormit replied.

"Diormit, I will tell you a secret if you promise not to reveal it."

"Of course, Father."

"The Lord calls me. My life will end by the middle of this night."

Diormit began to cry, and Colmcille tried to comfort him as much as he could.

On his way back to the monastery, Colmcille rested by the roadside. A white horse that was used to carry milk to the monastery approached the saint and put its head on Colmcille's chest.

"Get away!" Diormit shouted.

"Leave the horse be. Can't you see that it is saying goodbye? Look at the tears it cries. God has revealed to this poor creature that I am going away."

Colmcille blessed the horse and it walked away sadly.

The saint then went back to his hut and wrote a copy of the psalms.  After attending church, he returned to his hut and rested.

Then he said his last words: "I commend to you, my little children, my last words. Love one another wholeheartedly. Peace."

Later that evening the bells rang for midnight prayers. Colmcille reached the church before the other monks. As he knelt at the altar to pray, a heavenly light shone around him for an instant and then it was gone. The church was in darkness. Diormit ran to where Colmcille was lying at the altar.

The other monks entered with lamps and gathered around.

Diormit helped Colmcille raise his right hand to give the monks a final blessing. Then the saint opened his eyes wide, smiled and died peacefully.

On the night of his death, groups of fishermen in Colmcille's home county of Donegal claimed that they saw the whole sky light up as a large pillar of fire shot up into the sky, lighting it up as if it was daytime.

Colmcille was wrapped in fine cloths and after a funeral that lasted three days, he was buried. His first cousin Bóithín took over the role as Abbot of Iona.

*Life after Colmcille*

The monastery in Iona continued for many more years. The Book of Kells, a Latin illustrated manuscript of the four Gospels, once called "the most precious object in the Western world" was created around the year 800 by monks who originally came from Iona. They had left after being attacked by the Vikings, and settled down in a new monastery in Kells, County Meath.

Colmcille's feast day is June 9th, the date he died. Today he is regarded as one of the most important Irish saints. He was a remarkable person who helped to forge a close link between Ireland and Scotland. He loved Iona and he loved Ireland.

He wrote:

*Delightful to me to be on an island hill,*
*on the crest of a rock*
*that I might often watch the quiet sea*

*That I might watch the heavy waves*
*Above the bright water, as they chant*
*Music to their father everlastingly*

*That I might watch its ebb and flow in their course,*
*That my name should be – it is a secret that I tell –*
*"He who turned his back upon Ireland".*

# The End

# Word Sounds

*(Opinions may differ regarding pronunciation)*

| Words | Sounds |
|---|---|
| Cenél Conall | Ken-ale Ko-nal |
| Eithne | Ethna |
| Fedelmid | Fedel-mwid |
| Crimthann | Krim-han |
| Cruithnechán | Krith-neh-kawn |
| Dalriada | Dal-reed-ah |
| Diarmait MacCearbhaill | Deer-mit Mac-Kare-vill |
| Curnan | Kur-nan |
| Diormit | Deer-mit |
| Leac na Cumha | Lack na Kooah |
| Áedán | Ay-dawn |
| Eochaid Buide | Yuck-id Bwee-dah |
| Colmán | Kull-mawn |
| Druim Cett | Drim Ket |
| Filidh | Fill-eh |
| Bóithín | Bow-heen |

# ORDER ONLINE from poolbeg.com

Available Now

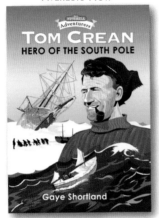

**Tom Crean**
Hero of the South Pole
*by Gaye Shortland*

Coming Summer 2018

**Amelia Earhart**
Adventurer and Aviator
*by Ann Carroll*

Coming Summer 2018

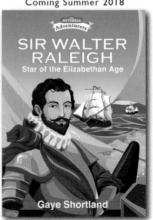

**Sir Walter Raleigh**
Star of the Elizabethan Age
*by Gaye Shortland*